A JOURNEY TO THE MIDDLE

How I embraced mediocrity and failed to turn my old vacuum into a rocket ship

BRADLEY POORE

T. Willingham Publishing

Ann Arbor, MI

First edition, 2021

For my daughter—don't just dream, act.

Thank you to both Sarahs, for helping me along the way.

Contents

Prologue

This is a book of essays, and while not all are true, many are. When I could not remember someone's name, I gave them an ambiguous one, and in one case I chose not to use a person's real name.

I am often told that I write like I speak. This does not bode well for you, the reader, so thank you for picking up this book and trying. Please know that I, and others, have worked hard to translate the firehose of gobbledygook that exits my brain and has ended up on the page. Again, I thank you—you are a brave soul.

What lies ahead:

You will find no real answers in this book. No secrets will be uncovered.

If you have made it to the middle, welcome.

If you are striving to get here, *do not give up*.

We have an open-door policy, and do not discriminate.

The middle is quite pleasant; the middle is cozy.

A Journey to the Middle

My journey to the middle.

For every dime you've earned, I've earned a nickel.

When you received an A, I got a C.

We passed each other on the street, but you didn't see me.

I am quite average, don't you know?

There are no awards in this life to bestow.

If you choose to come along for the ride,

I can assure you fun is never implied.

So, thank you, and I hope some of this makes you laugh.

As for the money you have spent, I promise to only waste half.

Cast of Characters you will encounter

Brad – *me, the author, mid-forties, married, kid*

Brian – *brother*

Sharon – *mother*

Gary – *father*

Mike - *HS Assistant Principal*

Adam - *roommate in Colorado*

Valerie - *gal from Boulder*

Ronnie Maddox– *neighborhood friend*

Daughter – *daughter*

Corvette – *1978 Corvette*

Chevette – *POS car*

Unknown Name of Lady - *lady my dad dated*

Unknown Name of Kid - *son of lady my dad dated*

Unknown People - *guys in pickup truck*

Tom – *friend from high school (deceased)*

Mary – *stepmother*

Clint – *Mary's son*

Chris – *the guy went by another name*

Buster Poindexter – *David Johansen*

Charlie Brown - *fifty grade teacher*

Johnny Carson - *Johnny Carson*

Dawn – *Borrowed her car (deceased)*

Dave #1- *guy riding shotgun (only story he appears in)*

Michigan State Trooper - *playing himself*

Brian S. - *bandmate in The Swedish Bikini Team*

Restroom Poets - *Brian, Ben, Jason, Chris #2*

Blues Brothers - *a movie about two brothers who play the blues*

High School - *Adrian High school (Adrian, MI)*

Colleen - *HS girlfriend & first wife*

Jeremy - *guitar player I went to HS school with*

Tim – *lifelong friend, musical partner, motorcycle travel companion*

Coffee Shop – *Bearclaw in Clinton, MI, now closed*

Matt - *friend who wrote the story about me*

William - *maternal grandfather*

Brighton Hospital - *adolescent substance abuse treatment center*

Thelma - *maternal grandmother*

Florida - *Sarasota, FL*

World War II - *it was a really big war*

Adam - *friend from HS and roommate in Boulder, CO*

Boulder - *it's a town in Colorado*

KBCO - *radio station 97.3FM*

Arapahoe Bason - *ski resort, "A-Basin"*

Mystery Machine - *hippie van*

Fred - *Fred Jones*

Shaggy - *Shaggy Rogers*

Scooby-Doo - *talking dog, pet of Shaggy, speech impediment*

Bob Ross - *painter, Air Force Veteran, awesome afro*

Dave #2 - *different Dave than before, same Dave as in "Is it principles or am I an ass?" former co-worker*

Matt – *longtime friend of Dave #2, collected $ for NOLA trip*

Beignet - *fried dough food*

The Guy Who Spent All the $ at the Strip Club - *I shouldn't...*

Ryan - *friend from HS (deceased)*

Evon - *paternal grandmother*

Sarah - *wife*

John - *not his real name (incarcerated)*

Dave #3 - *this Dave is my cousin in "I Blame My Cousin"*

Rick - *not a prick, resurfaced friend from HS*

Tiffany - *girl in hot air balloon who said "no"*

John - *guy in hot air balloon who proposed*

Shaun - *not her real name*

Spirit Animal - *unknown*

PART ONE

The True

Should be taken as accurate

Sandman

The only memory I have of kindergarten is when I brought one of my brother Brian's Star Wars figures to school. Honestly, it's my only memory.

It was one of the Sand People, who likely had a weird Star Wars name, like Gwan Kantankerin.
But maybe he was just a generic Sand Guy.
Or Sand Gal?
Can we apply a "they" in this case?
It could have been a Jawa.
I don't really remember; I was a child.
I ended up burying this action figure in the corner of the sand box.
I found the perfect spot for him to hide.
Dug a hole and put him inside.
My plan was to hide him until the following day and then dig him up.
Half days of kindergarten in those days.
I didn't ask Brian if I could borrow the guy.
Gwan wasn't there the next day.
Some other kid got a free Star Wars toy.

9

He was taken to a different home to battle their Star Wars crew.

My brother was annoyed I took Gwan and then lost him.

I wonder if he has forgiven me?

I wonder if he still remembers?

Maybe I should buy one off eBay for $80.

Give my brother back a Gwan, though, not *the* Gwan.

I don't like the sound of that.

One last thing:

Yes, I know the Star Wars figure I am telling the story about is actually called a Tusken Raider, don't be an asshole.

A Christmas Tale, Plus Some

It's Christmas evening, and I am reminded of something that happened many years ago, when I was a child. I was maybe six at the time, because my parents were still married. Brian had royally pissed off my father and consequently had all his Christmas presents taken away—shoved into a garbage bag and placed on the highest shelf in the garage.

This story got me thinking about some other knee-jerk reactions I have observed in my life, one of which happened in high school. It was on the day of an exam in biology class. The teacher was out for the day, so the assistant principal was sitting in for her. He and I had had a few run-ins in the past, so what went down was hardly a surprise.

We were in the middle of the exam when a friend who was sitting next to me did something to make me let out a faint chuckle. The assistant principal called my name and told me to turn in my test because I was done. I did what I was told and went back to my seat. I got a "what the hell happened" look from my friend; my response was a shrug. Before I could give it any more thought though, I was kicked out of class and the assistant principal told me to go down to his office and wait for him. When he finally showed up, he just sent me on to my next class. Something like this would have never happened if I had just continued to skip school. I began to think a dark cloud was following me around.

When my biology teacher returned, I explained what had happened, and the people who sat near me assured her I had done nothing wrong. She let me finish my exam. An F-U to the man, I guess. In a funny coincidence, I ended up spending some time with this man years later and was forced to call him by his first name, instead of Mr. Assistant Principal Sir; he was dating my first wife's mother. He actually gave us a very nice wedding gift. I should have called it even, but I couldn't; my grudge couldn't be stifled for a $500 check.

So, back to Christmas, since that was the original point. My brother did eventually get his gifts back. My father was the knee-jerk reactionary type, and thankfully my mother hated him, so she usually tried to undo his consequences, which were too swift and the kind that sometimes-caused physical pain. That, she couldn't undo.

That was the kind of stuff that happened in my house; that was the kind of stuff that happened in school. In these circumstances, I don't know if the punishment was deserved, or not. When the indiscriminate consequence wheel is spun, sometimes it lands on your name and sometimes it doesn't.

"Mom, Have You Seen My Bike?"

I was twenty-one and living in Boulder, CO. The night was just beginning, and the double date was too. My roommate Adam was talking about who knows what, when he launched into a story from my childhood. He was on a first date with his girl, while I was several in with Valerie, a girl I met through a mutual friend. Valerie was originally from Boulder but went to school at Wake Forest back east. She had come home to Boulder for the summer, and we hit it off right away. She's too smart for me, and while I love to listen to her spit out the medical jargon she was studying, I was out of my league.

Adam began to haul me kicking and screaming into his "getting to know you" part of the date. He turned to me and said, "Brad has this great story about his dad selling his bike when he was a kid." While this essentially told the whole story in one sentence, it also tended to provoke a sympathetic response from the listeners. I guess I would take what I could get at this point. I took his bait, took a somber tone, and went:

When I was around seven my friends and I were chatting on the bus home from school. We had some big plans, bike riding. What else is there really for seven-year-old boys besides throwing rocks at shit and riding bikes around? After hopping off the bus at the entrance to the neighborhood, we each headed home to get our bikes and were going to meet back up at the end of the boulevard.

There was a problem, though—dammit if I couldn't find my bike. I checked the garage, no bike. Checked the back porch, no bike. Back to the garage to check every nook and cranny, no bike. I headed into the house to ask my mother if she had seen it, thinking it must be somewhere. "Bad news," she tells me, "your dad sold it."

"Wait, Dad sold my bike?" I exclaim. That is a hard thing to comprehend when you're a child. Not sure I can comprehend it now. What kid doesn't have a bike? Or, more importantly, what kid has a bike, which is then sold by their parent, leaving them with nothing?

This, of all the things my roommate could bring up to talk about. How was this good date conversation? Maybe he was secretly using it as a dating sociopath meter? I honestly never understood, and I am pretty sure this wasn't the last time he did this to me. For those like Adam who grow up in happy, stable homes, the inverse must come off as entertaining. Put a quarter in the slot and the sad monkey will perform.

Sorry About the Door

You told me I was too small for the tractor.

And perhaps my age should have been a factor.

You ignored all my requests,

until you finally said "yes."

It was a little scary to drive.

I might not make it out alive.

I did not really want to mow,

just to drive it round back, nice and slow.

As I pulled up to the porch,

I had it lined up, of sorts.

I stopped on the slab, a huzzah was in store.

Then I let my foot off the brake and I crashed through the door.

On Thin Ice

Growing up, I had a neighborhood friend named Ronnie Maddox. He lived a few houses down from me, and while I would have never called him my best friend, we would hang out from time to time and always got on well.

When we were teenagers, he ended up being the guy who would show up at our party only after everyone else had gone home. In Ronnie would stroll, with a cigarette in one hand and Jack Daniels in the other. While we were cleaning up, he would just be getting going. He was soft spoken, yet visceral, which made him seem a little unpredictable even to me, and we had spent a lot of time together since childhood. He seemed pretty hardcore to the guys who didn't know him. How many teenagers just wander into a party at 3 a.m. and are ready to throw-down like a Japanese businessman?

As children, we played outside a lot. Our neighborhood was outside of town and adjacent to a large wooded area. We had hundreds of acres to explore, and we tried hard to explore every part of it.

One winter, we were out exploring, and while making our way back home we found ourselves needing to cross a creek, or two.

We were crossing a small creek that was frozen over. This was something we'd done so many times. and it seemed harmless enough. What happened next taught me a life lesson, and gave me nightmares for decades.

Ronnie was crossing the creek first—he put one foot onto the ice and plunged straight down. One second, he was there; then, nothing. It felt like time stopped. My memory has me remembering it like a magician's trick—there was the slight pause built in for dramatic affect after the initial disappearing. Or maybe it was like throwing a child's toy in the bathtub, how it goes under for just a fraction of a second and then it's back to the surface.

After he came back to the surface, I remember helping him out and running like hell home. Today, I can still feel the terror. My daughter knows this story well, because it gets repeated every winter, as well as whenever we're near any frozen water that isn't going into my cocktail.

"Remember that story I told you about Ronnie Maddox?" I always say.

"Is that the one about your friend falling through the ice?" she'll reply.

After I roll my eyes at her, she usually says, "Tell me again, Dad."

Thanks, but No Pie

This is another one of those stories that would amuse my friends and extended family. It is commonly referred to as the "Rhubarb Pie Incident."

When I was a child, my mom drove us around in her 1978 Chevrolet Corvette in the summer. People often refer to parts of Michigan as only having two seasons: winter and construction. So, here's where we introduce my mom's winter vehicle: the Chevrolet Chevette. The Chevette was a car created to compete with the small Japanese imports that were now available in the U.S. The difference was, compared to those imports that were flooding the market, the Chevette was a terrible car.

I digress—back to the Corvette. The Corvette was essentially a two-seater: two in the front and a clamshell in the back, which was flat other than a couple small cubbies built into the floor, one of which was useless because it housed the car's battery. Back in the late 1970s and early 1980s, children could ride in the front seat, or even in the back of a Corvette.

On this particular day, my mother had baked a rhubarb pie. I don't have memories of her being much of a baker, or even a cook, so this must have been a special occasion. Maybe it was the one pie my mother would bake all year? I was entrusted with watching over the precious cargo while stuffed in the back of the Corvette. I was not ready for the responsibility.

We lived in a small town, so it was ten minutes to any of our relative's houses. Ten minutes—*I could do this.* However, unfortunately, shortly into our journey, tragedy struck: a hard right, and it was over. Literally.

So, when rhubarb is in season, do not bring up rhubarb pie, do not offer me rhubarb pie, and do not tell me how delicious it is a la mode. Fuck rhubarb pie.

No Veg

A story of commitment and respect

When my brother and I were growing up at our mom's house, our diets were terrible. I'm talking Lucky Charms for breakfast, Fruity Pebbles for brunch, McDonald's for lunch, Eggo Waffles for an afternoon snack—you get the idea. There were *no* rules about nutrition in our home. The only vegetables we allowed on our plates had to be smothered in a delicious gravy or deep fried; they needed to resemble a food belonging to a completely different food group.

On the rare occasions my brother and I stayed with our father, though, he *had* rules. *How dare he!*, we thought. *Wait until we tell our mother you tried to make us eat an unfried vegetable.* And didn't he know that the only kind of oatmeal was instant? You know, maple and brown sugar, just add water. How do they get it to grow like that? A bush?

Shortly before my father met the woman who would later become his second wife/our stepmother, he was dating a woman who had a son that was older than me and younger than my brother. Let's say he was eleven. We had a meet-and-greet dinner one night, and while I can't recall the main dish, broccoli was served as a side. My brother silently grumbled about this abomination while our anti-veg hero was emerging across the table: the boy. He vehemently protested the broccoli, but his mom gave him the normal, "Oh, just try it" or the backup, "Just do your best." Obviously, the stakes *had to be raised.*

After the threats of "room!" and "no TV!" he tried a couple of pieces. However, he had a revenge plan, and it involved *maximum grossness.* He waited a minute, until the calm returned and the attention was off him. The boy then shoved his fingers down his throat to make himself puke the whole thing back up. Now, while I admired his commitment to this veggie revolt, it was fucking gross. He had managed to get a little up by the time his mom lost her mind and sent him away. He earned our respect that day, that boy. We were shown the way forward.

I don't think my brother and I saw either of them ever again. My father probably figured he had enough baggage with his two boys that he didn't need to add ad hoc puking to his troubles. I think of that kid sometimes when I am enjoying broccoli with my dinner, and then I immediately stop. Because, well, I'm eating.

Radar Love

(like the song)

When I was fifteen years old, my friend Ronnie and I "borrowed" Brian's red Chevy Cavalier. It was actually a rental, but dammed if I can recall why my eighteen-year-old brother had a rental car.

While Brian slept, I quickly hatched the plan and roped in my neighborhood friend. Looking back, there must have been some external factors that led us to do this, not just trying to joyride. Cigarettes, I'm guessing—one, or both of us, needed a pack. I was no stranger to driving. I would routinely borrow friends' cars to run errands for my other, slightly older, friends. Jake wants to come to the party but needs a ride? Send Brad. I was happy to do it. What teenager doesn't like driving around for little/no reason? Which leads me to take back what I said earlier about why Ronnie and I were going out in my brother's rental car. Hey, I needed practical experience behind the wheel. Driver's education wasn't too far off at this point.

So, Ronnie and I set out, with our first stop being one of the gas stations in town that would still sell cigarettes to underage folks. The Michigan law restricting tobacco sales to those over eighteen had been passed just the year before, and many businesses in my small town were a little slow to enforce it right away. Thankfully for us, these things take time.

There was no real plan after that. Ronnie and I would drive around a little bit and then head back. A couple of kids enjoying some lawless freedom. Until I ran that red light.

Most people do not mean to run red lights. I have seen it done on purpose, and everyone who rides motorcycles has likely done it, since the left turn lane rarely works for a lone biker. Usually, though, it's a split-second distraction and then it's just too late to stop. You let out an "oh, shit!" if you make it through unharmed and realize what you've done.

So, I ran a red light in downtown Adrian. It was around midnight in the middle of the week, so thankfully I didn't cause an accident. The small town I grew up in wasn't a lively kind of place. There are two small colleges, but still little to do once the sun goes down. Historically, the largest employers in the town were the hospital and the General Motors factory. By the time I entered high school, the factory was all but out of business, leaving many of the townspeople without jobs, hope, or anything productive to do. While some people were able to bounce to another small factory or machine shop, the majority slid into poverty, and blight crept into the town.

The racial tensions in the town couldn't be ignored either. I attended the only diverse elementary school, and I saw and felt it my whole childhood. Later, when Donald Trump won the 2016 election, it was no surprise to me. I grew up with people like this. Folks from small towns who saw their factories close and their rather well-paying, low-skill, no-higher-education-requiring jobs disappear. They were angry.

When I ran that red light, I saw no police, and in my distracted state didn't even see another car. I was wrong, and what followed would leave me baffled to this day. A car, or what turned out to be a large pickup truck, swung out behind me from the intersection I had just driven though. At first, I thought they were just annoyed by my moving violation; they flashed their high-beams at me, but it quickly escalated to where we could hear shouting, and then a thump as something hit the car. As I glanced over at Ronnie, we both understood that it would be a long night and that we were in agreement that under no circumstance would I be stopping the car. The chase was on.

I did my best to dodge the objects and insults as they were thrown our way. I took it as easy as I could in town, since speeding away would only bring us to the attention of whatever police might be out patrolling. I weaved through the city streets, hoping we would come off as more of a pain and not worthy of these locals' time, but this did nothing but encourage them. I was an unlicensed fifteen-year-old and didn't have many tricks in my driving bag. I had my hands full, and like a professional rally co-driver, Ronnie did his best to relay instructions as needed without unnecessary commentary.

We headed out of town for the country roads, because I felt like the new red Chevy Cavalier could outrun their pickup truck. I headed for the long, straight stretches that would allow me to end this nightmare I'd brought upon the two of us. When I finally got out of the city, I slammed my foot down on the accelerator and held it there. I needed every single mile per hour the Cavalier could give me—I needed out of this damn situation. Initially, this worked; the Cavalier flat out was pulling away from the truck, and we were on our way to ending this. But I just couldn't give them the slip. The bottle-throwing, racial-slur-yelling guys in the pickup were determined to get their hands on us. I was a fifteen-year-old kid who probably weighed 120 pounds fully dressed. I had little hope in the way of physically defending either of us.

With my plan of flat-out speed failing us, we had to rethink the strategy and try something else. As we drove back into the city and back onto the 35-mph, four-lane city streets, I did my best to maintain the speed limit while getting updates from Ronnie and trying to just remain calm. As they pulled alongside us to hurl insults (they appeared to be out of trash to also hurl), I had a new idea of how to end this.

As I drove along in the right lane toward the courthouse, I quickly relayed my new plan to Ronnie and then put it into action. At 35 miles per hour, I could slam on the brakes and turn right down a narrow street that ran around the back of the courthouse and ran adjacent to the Sherriff's Department and jail. I thought this could do a couple things: being adjacent to us in the left lane, they'd never make that right turn at speed and would either have to go around the block or pull into a business on the left side of the road and come back around that way. Or, if they knew the town, they would realize that Ronnie and I were heading straight toward the police station. Either way, it might encourage them to decide they'd had enough fun for the night and go home.

I slammed on the brakes and took the hard right, got the all-clear from Ronnie that they didn't seem to be taking any immediate action to follow us, stopped the car, spun it back around as quickly as possible, and headed back the way we came. When we didn't see the truck (whether because they decided to go around the block and cut us off or because they'd had enough, I'll never know), I immediately turned for home. Paranoid, nerves frayed, and sleep deprived, we lit up well-earned cigarettes.

I dropped Ronnie off, put the car and keys back where I had originally got them, and went to bed. Ronnie and I have never talked about what happened that night, and at least from my end, I never told the tale until now. Any blame for whatever took place that night fell squarely on my shoulders. I felt guilty for putting Ronnie through that ridiculous situation, and embarrassed for it happening in the first place.

In the end, the car was undamaged and so were we. A takeaway from this should have been me not driving again before earning my driver's license. However, it did nothing to deter me. I am a slow learner, and getting chased by locals in a pickup truck in the middle of the night apparently wasn't enough to keep me from illegally getting behind the wheel. Sad, but true. What would it take? That's another story.

A Moped?

I met this guy named Tom at a mutual friend's party. We smoked a joint and hit it off, though I don't believe much coherent conversing goes on amid smoking weed. He was one of those guys who made it feel like we had known each other always, even after just hanging out for a little while. I realized later that a lot of people felt that way about Tom—he was a likable guy and had a lot of friends.

I had to take off since I wasn't old enough to drive and my ride was heading out; we made plans for him to swing by in a couple days so we could hang out and get high again. I was not only hoping this meetup would occur, but I was also pinning my hopes on Tom being a bountiful and endless supplier of weed for me. A new friend and a new source—one hell of a night.

I had little to go on about Tom. Who was he? What grade was he in? There were a thousand-plus people in my high school that I only kind of attended, so it would be easy for us to have never noticed each other. I was betting on him being a senior. Since he did seem a little older than me and had said he would come over to my house, I assumed he had a car, which put him as a senior or maybe a junior. Over the next couple of days, Tom and I sorted out the hanging-out details, and he said he'd be over after swim practice. *Swim practice?* My new source was on the high school swim team? That was unexpected. Tom being on the swim team would later turn out to be beneficial, as swimmers get really good eye drops, which is a must if you're a teenage pot smoker.

I waited outside. I also had a mother who didn't come home from work until well after five, so we had plenty of time. The next thing I see is my new friend on a red Honda Spree coming down my road. Tom, as it turned out, was my age and in my grade. I had not guessed that. Sadly, our fun, our friendship, and his visit were all cut short. Not too long after Tom showed up, Brian came home. He told me we had to talk and that I needed to send Tom on his way. This was a strange request from any member of my family, but he looked serious.

My brother told me that he had talked with our mother, and not only would she not be coming home that evening, he wasn't sure when she would be coming home. He stated that after work she would be checking herself into our local hospital's psychiatric ward for an emotional breakdown/nervous breakdown, though as I now understand there is no such diagnosis in the DSM-V and those are more just umbrella terms used to describe more wide-ranging diagnoses. Brian was now eighteen and could legally take care of himself; I was still a minor and needed parenting, and quite badly I might add. This left little choice for me but to go live with my father, who would only begrudgingly take me in.

I began to pack a bag, not knowing how long I would be staying at my dad's. My father had only been remarried for a few years at this point, and my stepmother had a son from a previous marriage who was handicapped. I was seriously interrupting their family dynamic, and I was bringing plenty of emotional and physical baggage with me. Bag packed, my brother gave me a ride over to my new home.

I believe they did the best with what they were given. I was unruly and unhelpful, barely went to school, and generally spent all my time in my room listening to heavy metal. I wouldn't have welcomed me with open arms. I lived there for several months until they got tired of me and my mother was forced to either take me back or leave me on the street.

When you're a kid, there should be a place you can call home. I don't know if I ever had that. I had a room. I had stuff. But I never felt like I had a home. On a few occasions, I have driven by the house I grew up in, and I hold no fondness for it; it's just another building in another neighborhood that looks familiar.

Just Tell Me How Many Beers to Pour Over My Head

Another late night and another beer run. With no evidence to the contrary, I contest that my life would have turned out differently if I would have just skipped the beer runs. Why was I on them anyway? I couldn't drive, I couldn't pay; I only took up a seat in the back and added more cigarette smoke to the inside of the car. I probably even complained when they didn't come back with the kind of beer I liked. I'm sure they heard me, the fuckers.

Chris was driving and we were heading back to his house now that we were restocked and the party could continue. What no one knew was that Chris's car had a slight electrical problem—his reverse lights were stuck on. At midnight, driving down a dark road, those bright white reverse lights were easily spotted by the police.

We had about a mile to go to Chris's house when he was pulled over. Four underage kids, a case of beer in the trunk, and a driver who had been drinking. We were all pulled out of the car and told to line up. The police may have been bored or just wanting to get out of this with the least amount of paperwork possible. After talking it over for a minute, the two officers approached us with an idea.

Four teens, twenty-four beers—that makes six per person. Here was their pitch: each of us pour six beers over our heads, and we could go free.

I was all for the beer shower idea. "I could do more officer, if you'd like? Should I do twelve?" You see, I was already knee deep in the juvenile court system, and me getting caught out after hours for doing *anything* would likely land me in juvenile detention. "The whole case officer, please?"

My friends refused the officer's deal. I whispered to one of them that I was screwed if we went down for this, to which he replied, "Don't worry man, they're not gonna do anything." Um, really?

The officers went to their car to talk it over, and I silently freaked out standing there at the side of the road. I mean, the officers were probably in there laughing about how these privileged white kids were complaining about how their civil rights were being violated. Underage, white, drunk, high, and driving around with a case of beer in the trunk. Civil rights my ass.

But it worked. The officers came back and told us we could pour it all out on the side of the road and go home. *How* did that work? Maybe they were just bad police officers? I say that because the next decision they made was to have the guy riding in the passenger seat drive us the rest of the way home. The driver *had* been drinking, sure, but the passenger was on LSD.

"Sure thing officer, sorry to have bothered you this evening, we'll get those lights fixed."

We drove off. Is it white privilege that allows things like this to go on? Did the officers think they were in a tight spot once "we" turned down their offer? What if we did tell? Who would have cared?

And why was I on a beer run?

Buster Poindexter Is the Devil

My fifth-grade teacher's name was Charlie Brown. I can also remember fifth grade because it was 1984 and it was an election year. I remember Mr. Brown presenting the candidates to the class, and then we voted. Reagan won. Mr. Brown looked like the actor who played Mr. Kotter. When I think of him now, I'm pretty sure I am replacing what he *actually* looked like with that actor, Gabe Kaplan. Another interesting thing about Charlie Brown was that he told us how he had not broken a bone until he was around forty. "Then I broke all of my bones," he explained, when he was in a car accident. I am not a medical expert, but I assume if a person broke every bone in their body, they would not survive.

At forty-six, I have yet to break a bone. I have managed to avoid it despite years of skateboarding, downhill skiing in conditions well above my skill level, a motorbike crash in Memphis, TN, and plenty of downs and offs while racing my off-road motorbike. I have not played it safe by any means, and yet I have come out by-and-large physically unscathed.

Another feather in my cap is that I have been relatively healthy over the years. There is something known as *The Streak* to those who are close to me. This revolves around me and the act of throwing up. I have a distinct memory of the last time I was sick. As a teenager, I had been battling a terrible cold and was prescribed cough medicine. Whoa, mama, did I take too much. I guzzled a goblet full of medicine and crashed on the couch. Smart, right? I woke up to Johnny Carson interviewing Buster Poindexter. While that alone is strange enough, the fact that Buster was glowing while chatting with Carson *did not* seem right. Buster was the devil incarnate. I then ran to the bathroom and threw up. This was when The Streak began!

I tried to replicate this a couple nights later, minus the throwing up part. Mixing the cough medicine with alcohol, pot, and cigarettes only made me feel like shit. The Streak is real; it has now been thirty years and counting.

Just to throw this in at the end: In doing research into making sure I spelled Buster Poindexter correctly, I was surprised to find out that I knew more about him than I originally thought. Buster's real name is David Roger Johansen, and he was one of the original members of a punk band called New York Dolls. While I was familiar with the band, I didn't make the Buster Poindexter connection until writing this book. This is neither here, nor there. Just wanted to pass it along in case you didn't know.

I'm Sober Officer, I Swear

Another story about a beer run, with a totally different
outcome

I

When I was fifteen, I was stopped for speeding. I was
driving my friend Dawn's car, coming back from
getting beer with my friend Dave. Those first two
sentences are an absolute mess and a minefield of bad
decisions. The story is simply about how a dumb kid
thought he was smarter than the devil perched on his
shoulder.

I had been swiftly overtaken on a busy, five-lane,
50-mph speed limit road that was leading us back to
where the thirsty partygoers were. Being ignorant, I
decided to pursue. I did not catch the other car. I
caught the eye (and radar) of a Michigan State Police
Trooper. We were pulled over. Being fifteen and
speeding were somewhat minor issues compared with
the fact that I had been drinking, albeit a little earlier in
the day. Not a lot, mind you, but enough.

I complied and pulled the car over, well within view of my friends, who were rightfully concerned. Their beer could be at stake. God was chuckling at the devil on my shoulder.

Smelling like cigarettes and beer, I was immediately asked to step out of the car, and the Trooper began a series of tests to determine my sobriety. I walked the line forward *and* backward, I had to do the alphabet forward and thankfully *not* backward, and the last was to hold my arms outstretched to the sides, bend at the elbow, and touch my nose. None of these was a real challenge sober, which I thankfully was. How glad am I that this was before the days of smartphones? All my friends would most definitely have had their phones out and zoomed in, recording my sobriety tests.

The beer I'd had was some time before being pulled over, so while I may have smelled like alcohol and smokes, I *was* able to pass the Trooper's tests without too much difficulty. I then joined the State Trooper in his car so he could get all my info. Here is when morality comes into play, wondering if I could even get myself out of this situation. I was tired of getting a ride home from the police, or worse needing a ride home from jail.

II

I lied. Between the time I finished the tests and when I sat down in the passenger seat of his cruiser, I had figured out how to get away. I was going to be my older brother, and being very apologetic, I had walked off and left my wallet at my friend's house, to where I was returning immediately after we were finished. "Sorry officer, stupid mistake," was the best I could muster, as I was trying not to think about the beer in the trunk and what the long-term consequences were going to be for this lie I'd just told. Always later.

A speeding ticket for ten over and a ticket for driving without *my* license, and I was turned loose. I climbed back into the car, and Dave was white as a sheet. "Don't ask," I said through gritted teeth.

"How the fuck did you get out of that?" was Dave's reply.

"Later," I said as I pulled my seatbelt on and started the car. Always later.

45

A couple of hundred yards down the road, to everyone's amazement, I pulled into the driveway. The beer was being delivered and the party was once again going. I also assured Dawn that everything was fine with her car and not to worry. My guess is she was watching the action, waiting for a tow truck to show up and take her car away.

My decision to impersonate Brian would have some long-lasting consequences. Once the ticket had been issued, there would be only a couple of weeks before it would need to be paid, and I had no money. With time running out, I had to approach my brother and beg for him to take the bullet for me. I was delusional. My brother had no intention of doing that, and he let me know I had no choice but to deal with this situation head on and brave the consequences that would surely follow.

III

We contacted the officer and explained the situation. He then drove over to the house to re-issue the ticket to me, and add the whole driving-without-a-license bit.

The officer asked Brian, "So how do you feel about what your brother did?" I could tell the officer was not happy about being lied to and having to come over to our house to rewrite the ticket. When my brother failed to give the Trooper a satisfactory answer, the officer again baited him: "I'd be pissed off if my brother did this to me." Again, Brian didn't take the bait; he understood the shitstorm that was currently swirly around me and probably had a little sympathy. (I cannot think of a better description than shitstorm. It seems appropriate.)

The party I was attending that day was to celebrate the end of the school year. What was supposed to be my sophomore year, to be exact. It also coincided with was me getting off juvenile probation for the first time in a year, and free from the Lenawee County Juvenile Court system. Only, I wasn't free. I had been released by my probation officer a few days prior, who informed me that if nothing happened, I would be released within a week.

I did not make it a week.

After the call was made to the State Police Trooper informing him of my tomfoolery, a call was also

47

placed to my juvenile probation officer to give him the bad news. I'm guessing my files weren't even put away. A choice was presented to me: six months in a juvenile detention center, or a month in a substance abuse treatment center. A choice, they called it. Is that really a choice?

IV

Less than a week later, I became a resident of Toledo Hospital's adolescent drug and alcohol treatment center for the next twenty-eight days. There is a theme that runs through a lot of my stories: me being invisible. I discuss the positive and negative sides of this, and when it came to being in rehab, this character trait (or whatever it is) came in handy.

There is no easing into rehab. On my first day, I was put in with another new kid who refused to go to dinner, or group, or participate in any way. By the next morning, he was dragged away, kicking and screaming. The rumor was always that when kids left like that, they were sent to the psychiatric ward. I can't verify where any of these kids actually went when

48

dragged away. It happened a couple times during my stay, and it scared the shit out of me.

Rehab is monotonous. That *is* part of the point. You take teens who have had no structure, set them to a schedule, and hope wonderous things will happen. In its simplest form, it is a fine idea, but if you are expecting teenagers who have had little parenting or structure to suddenly turn their lives around, it's folly.

Change in the household can't happen from bottom, it needs to be top down. Maybe our parents should have been in *parenting rehab* for twenty-eight days instead?

Eat, group, free time in your room, group, eat, outside time, exercise, group. That is your day/week/month. I was well liked, and I drew sympathy from staff for being sent away from my mother's home to live with my father, who then sent me back. There was an instance in group where the counselor was grilling a kid about his home life and how good he had it. "Ask Brad how it feels to have nowhere to go," he proclaimed. "You have a warm bed to sleep in," he continued. "It feels bad, doesn't it?"

He was looking at me now; they all were. I nodded in agreement. "You're fucking lucky," he told the kid. "You remember that." The counselor tapped me on the shoulder after group and told me he was sorry if he upset me by bringing up something so painful. Truthfully, I did not give a shit. If staff wanted to feel bad for me for not being loved by my parents, I would take it. *Keep your head down and count the days,* I told myself over and over.

For good behavior, I was allowed to have my guitar in my room. I had been playing for around a year, and it was my real passion. I practiced every second we had downtime, because I had been invited to play with an actual band at a Battle of the Bands competition with my brother, a couple of his musician friends, and a singer who I knew from school. They mailed the songs I would need to learn to the rehab center, and I worked on them, hard. *A real band!*, I told myself. I would be playing rhythm guitar and just basically filling in the gaps, musically. Now I had three things to do: keep my head down, count the days, and play guitar. Maybe rehab *wasn't* so bad.

The days fused together. The rehab kids attended some Alcoholics Anonymous meetings and Narcotics Anonymous meetings, we went to parks during the day, we did our exercises outside on lovely summer afternoons, we played foosball, and some of what they were telling me started to make sense. I could understand the principle of it, and I liked the comradery, which I had never felt from my family, or school. The twelve-step programs did not turn people away; everyone was given a chance to speak, and you could smoke *and* drink coffee. I was starting to like being an alcoholic.

I even heard from a guy at one of the meetings that sometimes there would be donuts, or cookies. Now, I was hooked. A warm place to smoke, drink coffee, eat donuts, and complain about how your parents have wronged you? I would have skipped drinking alcohol and doing drugs if I knew a place like this existed.

When my twenty-eight days were up, I went home, probably with a participation trophy. After a little while, the twelve-step meetings wore on me, and I could no longer listen to everyone's woes. I would make a terrible therapist.

Rehab had helped alter my attitude enough to keep me out of trouble from here on out. So, I think that *is* enough to call it a success. Honestly, if my probation officer had just sent me to Antigua for twenty-eight days, that would have worked too.

V

Several years later, I was driving home from skiing in northern Michigan when I was pulled over for some mild speeding on that same road. Hands on the wheel, license, registration, proof of insurance—I knew the procedure by now. When the Michigan State Trooper returned with my information, he said with a chuckle, "have you been drinking tonight Bradley?" I then realized that in an amazing coincidence *this* was the same Trooper that had pulled me oven when I was fifteen. To his credit, he didn't write me a ticket. This must be part of what separates a good police officer separate from a bad one. He didn't hold a grudge for my lying and wasting his time years earlier. He sought no petty revenge by writing *me* a ticket that night.

This seemed like a kind gesture, which made me rethink my view of the police. I guess they were not all dicks. I know I would have given me a ticket.

Fence and Fog

I played this gig one night in Toledo, OH, when I was sixteen. I was in the band opening for my brother's band, The Restroom Poets. I was one half of an acoustic act called The Swedish Bikini Team. I believe it derived from an early 1990s, terribly sexist American beer ad involving scantily clad women. Just for the record, Brian S. and I did not wear bikinis on stage. It was just a name we thought was funny.

After being let in through the front, we dragged our gear up to a second-floor bar, and it was a sight to behold. First off, the place was empty—no bartender, and not even the guy who had opened the door for us was around anymore. It was also a nice place—the large, four-sided bar had a diamond-plated top. For those who may be unfamiliar, diamond plate is the same stuff truck boxes for tools and such are made of. The next thing we noticed was the stage, which was mostly surrounded by a chain-link fence, floor to ceiling, with openings on either side around six feet wide. It reminded me of The Blues Brothers movie when they played a gig in a Country *and* Western bar.

Maybe this place *was* a Country music bar; I never found out to the contrary.

With no direction, we got ready for the show and set up our gear behind the fence. We patiently waited for the time to start, and when it came, we just started our set. We waited for someone, anyone to show up, but no one did. We started to think this might just be an audition for the bar's management to see if we were worth having in and promoting, but with no staff even around, we were at a loss. This would not be the last time I played music only for the friends who rode along to the gig and had nothing better to do that night. We played a typical set and did our best, but my partner decided we needed a little help on the last song. Brian S. asked a couple members of The Restroom Poets to join us on stage, because unbeknownst to me, he wanted to put on a grand finale. He put down his guitar during the song and proceeded to climb up the fence, which to my relief was quite sturdy. He spent a good deal of the last song ten feet up, and it was one of the more memorable things a bandmember of mine has done.

We ended our set and moved our gear off the stage, and The Restroom Poets set up. Once they were ready, they just started their set. After they had started, my bandmate and I realized the level of the mic was too low. For our acoustic duo, it was fine, but once a whole band started playing, you could not hear the singer. With no soundman on site, we had to do it.

After a minute, we located a staircase around the rear of the stage, and at the top was the large mixing board, which to most people would have looked like a console in a nuclear missile silo. This was straightforward though, since everything was down except the main vocal. We made the change and they were back up and playing. As we looked at all the switches and sliders, we noticed there were controls for the lights, and the most wonderful live music effect ever: a smoke machine.

We pressed the button on the smoke machine, and *it worked!* Looking back, maybe I should have apologized in advance for what was inescapable. We ran the lights for the rest of their show and waited for the final song. The smoke machine was now unleashed. My partner mashed the smoke machine button as I pushed every button and flicked any switch that had to do with lighting. We found out that day that we couldn't be trusted with such power.

The song ended and the smoke permeated the bar. I could no longer see the band, which was maybe fifteen feet away. Around this time, two guys who worked for the bar showed up, with one remarking, "Guess you guys found the smoke machine." We all had a laugh, and then we essentially packed up all our gear and left.

Thus ended one of the stranger nights of my music "career." Looking back at that night, I am not even sure if all my story *is* true. We had asked around when we played other shows in Toledo about the bar, but no one had ever heard of the place. We would describe the huge diamond-plated bar and the fencing around the stage, and we got back blank stares. It had been built for us, for that one night in Toledo, where the band was given command of the toys to use as they saw fit.

We were able to be rock stars, if only for a night.

My Senior Year That Wasn't

Part I

When I dropped out of high school for the second time, I was seventeen. I did the calculation of how many credits I would need to graduate, and it was hopeless. The year was 1992. For a while, I held out hope that maybe some deal could be worked out that would involve summer school, an extra class in the morning or the afternoon.

It turned out that no deal could be reached, no arrangement made for extra classes. No magic bullet. The truth was, why should there be? I had shown no real desire to better my station in school. I'd never really asked for help or special treatment; like a normal teenager, I just attended school. That was all I did. I had become more visible to my teachers and to the administration, because like the other 99% of students, I came to school. *Dammit, why was I not informed of how this worked from the beginning?* Maybe if I started getting all A's in my classes, I could then go and plead my case to the principle. I was an average student who was barely noticed on a day-to-day basis.

Being invisible can be delightful. You can hang out in the back of classroom and go unseen, which is helpful if you're coming to class high, have skipped a couple classes to do shots, or need some sleep since your head didn't hit the pillow until 3 a.m. because you were playing music in a bar in another state.

The disadvantage of being invisible to your teacher and the staff is that people get used to it. When someone *is* at school every day, the same assumption is implied. The teacher, your friends, whomever, just assume you will be there the next day, the day after that, and so on. When you're never there and suddenly you show up, the teacher and other students assume you'll soon be gone again.

I wanted to make this year count though. I stopped coming to school high, and I did my best to keep up with schoolwork, though I understood little of it. Years of ditching class were not only robbing me of a diploma, they had also made me ignorant of the knowledge that was needed to succeed in a traditional public-school setting. God dammit, I was going to try though.

I also became partially visible that final year via a romantic relationship with a well-liked, soccer-playing daughter of a doctor, Colleen. Much to her parents' dismay, she and I became inseparable. The poor girl should have been locked in a tall tower by her parents. They may have even tried that, but she just snuck out the front door when they were asleep. Colleen and I would marry several years later, and then divorce. But let's not focus on that.

Another positive aspect to my last year of high school was that my friends and I were given control of the music that was played at the two big assemblies that year. We were allowed to pick who played in the band and what songs were performed. This power was, of course, immediately abused. After the first assembly, we were given a talking-to about relaxing the exclusivity of our "club." We weren't pissed when our hand was forced, but we took umbrage at the fact that we were the best musicians the school had to offer. How dare they tell us we needed to hold open auditions for lesser talent? *This* did not sit well with the band.

I did not give this musical monopoly much thought until many years later, when my long-time music partner Tim and I were hosting an acoustic open mic night at a small coffee shop in Clinton, MI. A guy named Jeremy dropped in to say hi after playing a show up the road. Jeremy greeted me like we were old friends, and I later learned we had gone to high school together and had perhaps met? I didn't have a lot of friends in high school, so you'd think I would remember him, but I didn't. He was a nice guy, so I felt kind of bad. Again, in my defense, I didn't spend a lot of time in school, so I'm just as surprised he knew who I was.

We ended up giving Jeremy the last slot that evening, and we were actually in for a real treat. He was a far better guitar player than I could ever be. This wasn't talent that just manifests itself in your twenties—he must have been good back when we were in high school too. Shall I point out again how musicians are often dicks?

Who else did we exclude? Maybe Jeremy was like me in high school: invisible. If the roles were reversed, it would have been me sitting in the stands watching Jeremy play, wondering why no one asked me to play, thinking these guys on stage belonged to some exclusive club that didn't allow new members. Our exclusive club was just a band of misfits, and until now, outsiders ourselves. Our singer was now in his fifth year of high school; the other guitar player was a football player who quit football after joining up with us; my older brother had already graduated and was roped into playing bass guitar since we couldn't be bothered to audition any bass players who currently attended our school; and our drummer was the angriest guy I'd ever met. A couple years later, that same drummer accused me of trying to steal his girlfriend. As I remember, I lived in Colorado and they lived in Minnesota. Angry man, angry. This is all standard stuff for Rock & Roll though. It's amazing we didn't have any active drug addictions in the band.

Neither the girlfriend nor the band helped me academically, and my mediocre grades kept coming. As the year dragged on, I started to understand the consequences of all my past failures. *I would not graduate high school with my class.*

Toward the end of the school year, seniors were called out of class to do things like get measured for their cap and gown, and hell I don't know what else, *other stuff!* I was in a class with a couple seniors when one of these things happened. The time came, they were called out, and guess who didn't go? A couple people turned to me with looks of confusion. Someone near me said, "Why didn't you go?" I knew why. The jig was up, and this was the end of high school for me.

Immediately after school, I started figuring out my next move. I knew I couldn't sort this out overnight, but because I'd known this day was coming, I had some ideas. Family and friends rolled their eyes and did their best to humor me, but I was seen by most to be living in my own reality and devoid of any sense. What, my job at the pizza/sub shop was a dead end? Was my complete lack of motivation the issue? I stopped drinking alcohol and smoking dope all the time, wasn't that enough to prove that I could make some good decisions?

I spent the next week figuring out how to exfiltrate myself from Adrian High School and how I could craft a future for myself. I needed a GED and to take the ACTs; then I could get myself into any number of community colleges or lower-tier universities. So, on a typical spring day in what should have been late into my senior year of high school, I stopped going. No fanfare, no going down to the office and announcing, "This school has held me back for far too long; today is the day I reclaim my dignity, my right to choose, my honor!" I just woke up and decided that was the day. I had a plan.

My Senior Year that Wasn't

Part II

Shortly after I left school a friend gave me a copy of an essay that had been sitting on a teacher's desk. I don't know what possessed her to pick it up and read it, but I'm glad she did. The essay had been sent to The Detroit News, or the Detroit Free Press (my memory is failing me on which one it was), as part of a short story contest they were having. The essay was about me. It had been written by a friend I'd played music with a couple times named Matt.

I was in awe. Who thinks someone will take the time to write a tale about them? It was an honest impression of me, and perhaps that's why he never told me about it. Not mean or insincere, just honest. Perhaps that's why he didn't tell me of its existence— it might have been less objective.

The subject was me; the theme was that I seemed more gypsy than student. Matt saw me as a clever guitar player who would drift in and out of school as I saw fit, and generally lived by my own rules. I was a complete mystery to Matt, who saw me as someone who had chosen to live outside the norm, where Matt and his friends dared not tread. The guy who you go out and have a beer with, but wouldn't invite him over to your house for fear of what he might do. I can only hope Matt saw me as an individual—that would be the best compliment he could have ever given me.

I never did tell Matt I had read his piece. He had me figured out in the first couple paragraphs, and I loved it. Thank you, Matt.

No Call, No Show

When I was in my early twenties, my maternal grandfather killed himself. At that time in my life, my career was in social work; I was basically a glorified babysitter at an inpatient adolescent substance abuse treatment center, though when I talked about my job it sounded very important, as if I was a crucial part in saving these kid's lives.

On the day my grandfather died, I was busy saving lives by playing a rousing game of kickball. Nothing out of the ordinary happened on my shift (my team lost), and then I went home. Shortly after arriving home I received a call from my brother; he was the person to inform me my grandfather had died. The disappointment was that by this time, my grandfather had been dead many hours already, and all the while I was playing kickball with teenagers instead of mourning with my family.

My grandfather had been a successful businessman who decided to sell his half of the business to his partner and retire to Florida. I was around ten at that time. We visited as often as we could, and when I was a kid, I enjoyed seeing by him and my grandmother. There were times when he would hand my brother and me fifty-dollar bills and take us to Toys "R" Us. What kid doesn't like a grandfather like that? He was a fair man, but cold. Neither he nor my grandmother were the warm, touchy-feely kind of grandparents, like my father's folks had been. To show us love, they handed us fifties took us shopping and out to dinner. My grandfather also helped my mother with money for bills, and gave her a job at his company.

As an adult, I can see how this kind of "love" impacts and shapes people. If your children are struggling financially, it is understandable to lend them a hand. If your children are struggling emotionally, don't buy them a new roof or redo their landscaping; it doesn't help. I watched this play out over and over my whole life. Death does not undo our wrongs. If we aren't careful, we'll damage generations.

My grandfather had somewhat recently started to drink, heavily. He and my grandmother had moved back from Florida to Holland, OH just outside of Toledo. At the time, the family assumed this was so they could be closer to their children and grandchildren, but since it never felt like people had actual feelings for one another, I'm not so sure why they moved back. Maybe it was just to supervise what all the money they were still giving their adult children was being spent on. My grandfather's drinking had gotten so bad that the Christmas before he died, he just sat in his chair in the living room and babbled incoherent nonsense. This was when I realized that the whispers I had been hearing were actually only minimizing what was really going on.

Not long before he killed himself, my family had asked me for advice on how to deal with what was clearly alcoholism. This was well beyond my skillset. A self-destructive World War II veteran whose wealth was dwindling and whose only means of coping was though alcohol? I could not help. I babysat teens for about two dollars more an hour than I could have been making at the grocery store.

So, I ended up being the last to know; I realized that day that I would never understand my family. I have drifted away ever since, telling myself that their way was the wrong way, and choosing actual emotional love instead of the kind that is purchased would have to be my way forward. My way. The only way.

The Exploding Mystery Machine

When I lived in Colorado, my roommate Adam and I caught wind of an event called a cardboard derby sponsored by a local popular radio station KBCO. It was held at the Arapaho Basin ski resort, which was a couple hours away from our apartment in Boulder, where we planned to build our derby vehicle. It was summer when we heard about the event, so we had a couple of months to plan, gather supplies, and build. The only rules were the craft *had* to be built from cardboard, tape, glue, rope, and paint. If you wanted to build an aircraft carrier out of those items and you got it to the resort via a semi-truck, you could race it down the hill.

Adam and I quickly settled on making the Mystery Machine from Scooby Doo. It may have been settled by the fact that Adam made a good Fred and I could pull off a pretty convincing Shaggy—he being blond and broad, and I, tall and skinny. I was hopelessly inept at growing even the worst mustache, despite being in my twenties.

The scavenging of the cardboard started, and we did well. I had insider knowledge of where to get some vital pieces. Before coming to Boulder, I had worked at a carpet store, doing the mundane stuff nobody else wanted to do. One of the more fun things was driving a forklift, which I used to get the incoming rolls of carpet, delivered via semi. Because of this, I knew that larger carpet stores would have the huge cardboard tubes that are in the middle of the carpet rolls. They would be perfect for the internal structure of our Mystery Machine.

With tubes acquired from our local carpet store and cardboard boxes for the outer shell gathered up from the office supply store where I worked, we were ready to build. I am the kind of person who stares at a bucket of Legos for an hour and then builds a house, then takes it all apart and tries to make something else, and that also ends up looking like a house. I have no imagination in this area.

When we finished the Mystery Machine it had a striking resemblance to the box that gets discarded when you get a new fridge. After all the time spent building, we had a refrigerator box vaguely painted like the Mastery Machine. Christ, it was a sight.

Adam and I scoured the local Salvation Army store for our Fred and Shaggy outfits, and I ended up with a fantastic pair of brown corduroy bell bottoms. We also ended up printing and laminating an 8x10 picture of Bob Ross and placing it on the very front of our craft. That alone got us more attention than our wonky craft.

The big day came. We loaded our entry into Adam's SUV and made the trek to Arapahoe Basin. Adam and I had both grown up in Michigan and spent most of our lives in the rather flat Midwest. Once we were off the highway and onto the mountain roads that led to Arapahoe Basin, I think we both wondered if we'd made a mistake, or at least underestimated this event. The truth was, it was both. This was a big event, and I was frightened.

We checked in and placed the craft in a row, among the others. It was a parc fermé, with booze. Adam and I quickly made friends, thanks to Bob Ross, and we became deluged with beer. There were several Mystery Machines, and if we didn't have Bob Ross ours may have been the worst. This was the mid-nineties, just after Bob had died, and most people recognized him but could not come up with his name. They loved him, though.

Our kind neighbors were too kind, and my roommate was becoming quite drunk; by the time we started hauling the craft up the hill to the starting line, Adam was stashing all this beer inside our Mystery Machine. Something else that was becoming more obvious was the enormity of the hill we would attempt to scuffle down. My roommate was the smart one; I think we probably should have both been drunk for this stunt. The hill was the final two hundred yards (give or take) of a ski slope, which was divided into three lanes, but that was not all—two "jumps" ran across all three lanes, and you were going over them on the way down. Beer, anyone?

The organizers shuffled things around a little and we were put with two other Mystery Machines for the run. Three lanes, everyone goes at once, and whoever makes it to the bottom has lived a good life and is well-liked by the LGBTQ+ gods above.

We shoved off the from the top, like bobsledders in the Olympics. I was huddled in the front since I was lighter and wouldn't have that weight on the nose. We were moving! For a few seconds, I think it was going well—the cardboard craft was heading down a ski slope—but we were not to withstand the jumps. Or maybe I should say, jump. We hit the first one at maybe a 30-degree angle, and all hell broke loose.

The Mystery Machine was not only poorly designed and built, it was also bursting with beer cans: empty, full, partially full, and unopened. Our neighbors who had gotten my roommate drunk had given him enough beer to get three people drunk. Adam, not wanting to offend these generous folks, had just put them here, there, and everywhere.

We landed after hitting that first jump, and the craft burst apart at every poorly crafted seam. The hill was immediately littered with beer cans, cardboard, and both me and Adam. The Mystery Machine was dead, a violent and drunken death. We dragged it down the rest of the hill and discarded it next to the other crafts, made by fools, for fools.

This Isn't My Sunglasses Case

My buddy Dave (Dave #2) and I were in the international terminal at Chicago's O'Hare airport, fifty feet away from the TSA security check. My sunglasses still sat on my head from the journey over in the shuttle bus. "Give me a second, Dave, I need to put these away," I called out over the busy din of the terminal. I stepped to the side as to not get in anyone's way, grabbed my case out of my backpack side pocket, and opened it.

I just stood there in disbelief. What was I seeing? Putting away your glasses is about the most mundane thing you can do, and certainly not worthy of a multi-page story. Not this day. As I stood there rooted to the spot, staring into the case, I had a moment of clarity that reminded me that I was fifty feet away from security and there were drug dogs patrolling the terminal.

In my sunglasses case was a pipe, and a small amount of marijuana. I started to splutter, "But... what..."

Then a panicked voice next to me blurted out "What are you doing with that?"

This time I couldn't even get whole words out. "Wh... bu... fffff...."

"That's not yours" Dave said, "it's mine." I slam the case shut, because now I can also smell it.

Now I got it, we had the same sunglasses case; I must have grabbed his when we got out of the car instead of mine.

"Shit." I looked at Dave, and we were both puzzled.

"Man, that was a gift," he said, realizing he was about to lose it. We both knew that we didn't have time to take the shuttle back to the car, swap the cases, and still make our flight. I felt terrible, and stupid. "Chuck it," he said with a sigh. I casually wandered over to the nearest trash can and threw it in. When I got back to Dave, I pleaded, "I'll buy you a new one when we're in Ireland. I'm really sorry."

I offered to go into a couple different smoke shops when we were in Ireland and England so I could replace the pipe, but he wouldn't take me up on it. Whatever sentiment this pipe held, it obviously couldn't be replaced by me. I have yet to pay him back for having to throw his pipe away. What does it come out to with interest, I wonder? It has been twelve years since I threw it away in that terminal.

Call me crazy, but I do kind of wish I had tried to go through security with that. Would the look of shock on my face have been enough to not get me arrested? Does the TSA have compassion for idiots?

Embattled

I had a friend named Ryan who battled witches and evil spirits.

I was there when he went to war against the CIA.

I stood in amazement as he pitched the idea of an internet-connected sex toy to a patent attorney, long before any such thing existed.

I marveled at his spatter-painted VW Campervan he bought to drive around the country looking for Jerry Garcia.

I remained supportive when he did not find Jerry Garcia.

I cringed as he knocked on a stranger's door to ask to use their phone, which was all art of a plan he had to gain access to a particular house he believed to contain vast quantities of drugs. It did not.

I happily gave him my bicycle after finding out he had no transportation.

I was frightened the times he rolled his window down at stoplights to ask strangers if they had weed.

I was uneasy because he was unpredictable.

I was jealous of the voices in his head.

I was shocked that LSD could cause so much damage.

I felt puzzled by his schizophrenia.

I was sad when I heard he had died.

I was relieved for him when I heard he had died.

Ryan fought until the end.

The CIA won.

Is It Principles, or Am I an Ass?

Morning of departure:

It was 4 a.m. when the alarm on my phone went off. In my sleep-deprived state, I was a little confused at first about where the hell I was. After a couple seconds of blissful ignorance, I realized that I was on the floor—cold, hungry, sore, and shoved into a cramped corner in some strange bedroom. I quietly exhaled out a "fuuuuuuck" as I realized it was Monday morning and I was still in New Orleans. I needed to immediately get my ass up and call a cab to take me to the airport.

Then I was up and dressed, and everything I brought was haphazardly shoved into the backpack, which was all I came down here with. I didn't have a lot of time; I had to make that flight, because for some stupid reason I'd made the commitment to go straight into the office after my flight landed. Not a great idea, in hindsight.

The door to the rooftop deck was just a few feet away, so I went out to make my call. I pulled the number off a cab last night as I was staring at the Uber app, watching the prices rise and fall. Cabs were usually a flat fee to the airport, so that seemed like a good move. When I stepped out onto the deck, I was surprised to see someone was already out there.

Backstory:

I had flown down to New Orleans for a weekend bachelor party to celebrate my friend Dave getting married. I was last on the list; Dave didn't think I'd want to go. Lesson number 387—when an old friend tells you something like this, just send money and stay home.

I *am* a slow learner, which I have demonstrated a few too many times throughout this book. I really wanted to contribute to this in any way I could. I valued our friendship and thought this was a good way to show that. How bad could it be?

I got the itinerary from Matt, the guy coordinating the weekend. I sent him over my share for the house that was being rented, which according to him was half a block off Bourbon Street, the most touristy place in the city. I was beginning to worry. I purchased my flight; thankfully I was able to buy it with frequent flyer miles I had built up from recent business trips. New Orleans had been picked because it coincided with a concert by the band 311. I guess it's a thing the band does—they hold concerts every year on March 11. Get it? I let Matt know that I wasn't really interested in going to the concert, so he needn't buy me a ticket. "But everyone is going," was Matt's retort. I'd had enough of concerts. Matt's next question was, "But what are you gonna do all night while we're there?"

"It's New Orleans," I replied.

The weekend came, and I enjoyed my free flight, Uber ride to the house, and then I was there with the guys. It was a beautiful two-story home and, like Matt said, was half a block off Bourbon Street. There were nine of us in total, and the place didn't seem built to hold that many. Sleeping arrangements appeared to be an issue, and it nearly sent me into a panic. I seemingly had no bed, pillow, couch, or blanket at my disposal. All these things had been claimed before I arrived Friday evening. If I hadn't spent a couple hundred dollars on the place already, I would have bailed and gotten myself a room somewhere else. The company I worked for took care of us on the road, so I had grown accustomed to staying in nice hotels, driving nice rental cars, and being comfortable away from home. Another thing that struck me was that while many of the guys were around my age (early forties) I was the only one married *and* with a child. What the hell was I thinking?

I drank, I smoked; when the guys went to the concert, I immediately headed in the opposite direction of Bourbon Street and visited local art galleries. I had been to New Orleans a few months prior to this and found I really liked the city. The music, food, history, and architecture, the grittiness of it—I had just gotten a small taste of it last time and I wanted to see and experience more. After a good meal, I headed back, relaxed a little, and then turned in. I had settled on a dark corner in the upstairs bedroom next to the vanity. I scrounged a blanket out of a tiny closet that looked like it was a secret passage for a child, and I used my coat for a pillow. I had some difficulty sleeping, though, because two doors down was a large gay club, and the thumping bass that came through the walls was astounding. How could anyone live here full time?

I got back up for a spell after the guys returned from the concert, and a few of us went back out to grab a bite and a drink; I could do this for a couple of nights. After our short excursion, I headed for bed, around 2 a.m. Thankfully I am an early riser, so when I woke up the next morning, I walked down to Café Du Monde and picked up coffee and beignets for everyone. That might have been my sole contribution to the weekend.

The next night was concert number two, and it was basically a repeat of the previous night. They left and I wandered around, had a good meal, and lay down in my corner early while listening to thumping bass seep in through the headphones I had put on in a feeble attempt to drown some of it out. Again, they came back after the concert and I got up, hung out for a little bit, and then went back to bed. See, I told myself, I am fun. Kind of.

The last night came, and with no concert to attend, the guys were getting restless. We had spent a lot of the day hanging out at the house and chatting with passersby, giving tours of the house, enjoying the brass bands that walked by; the guys and I even stopped a barbershop quartet who had wandered too close and were given a treat when they performed a song just for us. I was loving the day. Like I said, though, the guys were restless, and like a match thrown onto gasoline, things were going to get out of control.

One of the guys mentioned going to a strip club, or clubs. They seemed to think this was a *must do* in New Orleans. I was at first relieved that there was not a consensus. The leaders of the call were determined, though—we all must go. I had said "no thanks" and was sticking with it. I thankfully had a couple of the guys who were on my team, but the opposition was strong and relentless. They fell, one by one, until there was only me. I was then fucking badgered for a good twenty minutes by the guys who said things like "it's okay. man, we won't tell your wife" and "c'mon, it's for Dave and it's our last night." The more they pushed, the more I was determined to stand my ground.

They did finally give up and leave—all of them. I have felt alone a lot of my life, felt invisible, yearned to be included, and then when I *was* included, I rejected it. This was no heroic show of devotion to my wife like a few of the guys assumed; I doubt, other than the complete waste of money, she would have minded. I had just made a decision that I felt was right, and didn't budge.

It ended up being another pretty nice night for me. I had another nice dinner in an Italian restaurant that was highly recommended, saw another part of the city I had not previous wandered into, gave a tour or two of the house to strangers, and then went to bed in my corner under the vanity. The boys returned and I hung out on the rooftop deck with them and listened to the strip club stories. I was tired and it was all so uninteresting I don't remember any of it, except that one of the guys wanted to go back to a particular club.

From the stories, he had spent a few hundred dollars at the club and "man, I know that chick liked me" types of stories were exiting his mouth in a drunken incoherent ramble. The guys were still trying to talk him into not going back and to just hang out when I gave up and went back to bed. I had to get up early to catch that flight.

Soon it was 4:03 a.m., and the fella who had spent all the money and was having common sense chucked at him by drunken buffoons was the person I found on the deck. Before I was able to make my call, he told me about how he did indeed go back to that club, found that same dancer, and before leaving the club had spent more than two thousand dollars. I was exhausted and only had calling a cab and getting out of there on my mind. I uttered a few "man, that's wild," and "wow, you must have had a good time," while he blathered on.

The taxi was only a couple minutes away, so I said my goodbye to only him and crept through the house and out the front door. "Two thousand dollars…" I muttered with a chuckle as I stood outside that house, hoping my cab would soon be there. I had a two-income household, and made a good living, and I couldn't figure out where I would just get two grand in cash to piss away. I think he worked an Amazon warehouse type job. Maybe I was in the wrong business.

On the plane ride home that Monday morning, I thought about what the hell had gone on over the last couple of days. Was it the inflexibility in my personality that caused me to alienate myself from the guys? They seemed happy to have me around, after all. On the other hand, I was able to explore a city that really intrigued me and have a couple of great meals.

I also wondered if I was an asshole. I doubt the guys walked away from the house the previous night feeling impressed that I had not given in in the face of unrelenting peer pressure.

I don't have an answer to the asshole question, though it's probably a matter of perspective. I did so many things in my younger years that I never wanted to do, some of which ended up being hard life lessons. I am glad I went, and I am also glad I did not back down. I am no longer a child seeking the approval from my peers.

PART TWO

The Shorts

Bermuda, Tweed, Cargo, Maternity, Board, Swim, Denim, Short, Too Short, Camo, Bike, Chino, Used, Pleated, Plaid, Leather, Running, Cut-Off, Linen, etc.

A Smash Hit

I was one half of an acoustic duo called The Swedish
Bikini Team, with my friend Brian S.

He made the decision to move from strictly acoustic
music to electric.

Think Dylan in 1965.

Not that good though.

Switching music genres when you are poor is difficult;
it becomes an upgrade cascade.

New this, new that. You almost have to sell off your
old equipment to buy the new.

So, I did.

Brian found a drummer and bass player.

My heart wasn't really in it.

Rock, or grunge, or alternative—it just didn't make
sense to me anymore.

I became an old folk musician when I was eighteen.

Brian wrote songs. We practiced. We were okay.

I secured us an opening spot, our first gig.

It was a favor from a high school friend of mine.

We played.

We were too loud.

The high school girls were a little frightened.

As we were coming to the end of our last song,

something interesting *did* happen.

We went from a mediocre alternative band to a bad

punk rock band.

Our bass player took it upon himself to smash his bass.

It was his only bass.

It was our first show.

He should have paced himself.

But it was hilarious.

Alone

I ran a 5K in my twenties. When I finished, no one was there to meet me.

I ran a 5K in my thirties. When I finished, no one was there to greet me.

I ran a 5K in my forties. When I finished, no one was there to treat me.

I didn't get first.

I didn't get last.

I tried hard.

I did my best.

If no one shows up to see you, did you do it?

Anyone See That?

I once got a tattoo that I thought was blue.

The problem is, I am colorblind.

The other problem was, the guy who did it was too.

I am told the color most resembles a crayon color

called "Purple Mountains' Majesty."

But what do I care? It's on my ass.

Close Enough for Rock & Roll

Okay, so I swear I used to say this when I was younger. Whether I ever said it out loud is another issue entirely. The one person I knew could answer this was Tim, a singer who I played with for many years, including my teens, when I was playing raucous music. When asked, he replied, "I have never heard that saying before."

This has to do with tuning your guitar. Rock & Roll is, um, noisy. At least it was the way my friends and I played it. It's so loud, in fact, that if you're not 100% in tune, no one may even notice, since your part is drowned out by the others.

Did I make this up? Maybe it was so long ago that no one remembers? Should I buy the URL? Have T-Shirts made? Can I copyright this?

CMG

My paternal grandmother used to cook me a dish
called chocolate milk gravy.
I cooked it once for my wife, to which she replied,
"God, that's shitty!"
I loved it too much.
So, I chose *it* over *us*.
And now I'm alone, and a bit weighty.

Tent Tickle

My friend Tom spent the night in a tent.

He died several years ago, so he need not consent.

To this story of glee.

While he was high on LSD.

It was something profound.

That I still can't get my head around.

We asked for wisdom from Tom.

And when called upon, he said,

"The only thing that matters is what's going on."

Death from Above

I heard somewhere Hugo Boss designed the uniforms
for the Luftwaffe.
I do remember them being quite stylish.
While none of this may be true, it is not stopping me
from telling everyone.
Am I lying if I don't care enough to look up whether
it's true?
Does it matter?
Will someone look this up and tell me if I am an idiot?

Didn't He Book a Show for Us Once?

I met this guy called John.

From the look of him, I thought he was a peeping Tom.

You couldn't believe the things he said.

He then did something that could not be undid.

To tell you the truth, his name wasn't John. I started writing this about a specific person; then I remembered what terrible things he did, so I decided to stop. I hope the bastard rots in jail, and when he's released, he is tied to a post in the town square and stoned by a group of randomly chosen women. Maybe I can organize a lottery for that? Let me know if you are interested.

I Blame My Cousin

I liked roller coasters when I was a kid, but my cousin Dave ruined it.

What did he do?

I was thirteen and at the local county fair with my family.

My cousin Dave knew the guy running a ride known as the Eyerly Spider, but most people just call it "That Spider Ride" or maybe "That Octopus Ride."

While Dave and I were on the ride, Dave encouraged "his buddy" to keep the ride going.

He did.

It did.

I almost threw up.

I kept my roller coaster riding to a minimum after that. Until 1993.

Until the Pirate Ship ride at Boblo Island Amusement Park.

It was nauseating.

It was regrettable.

I surrender.

I'm a Songwriter

I can't write pop songs because I am too angry.

I can't write country songs because my dog doesn't like me.

I can't write Christian music because I'm an atheist.

I can't write kids music because they don't like me.

I tried to write rock & roll songs but they seemed too loud, even on paper.

Classical music puts me to sleep.

Jazz does not make sense to anyone.

I think folk music has something to do with farming or camping, neither of which I do.

Just when I thought there was nothing left, a friend told me about sea shanties. So, I gave one a try:

> Six months at sea with no land in sight
>
> no women on board
>
> only men with which to fight
>
> drop the mains
>
> bring out the rum
>
> put on a pretty dress
>
> and fire the guns

After writing this, I changed my mind about the sea shanties. I decided show tunes are my calling.

Just a Normal Kid

Don't all kids:

> Refill their parents' vodka with water?

> Break into abandoned buildings?

> Steal money out of relatives' piggy banks?

> Walk 2.5 miles back home from school, immediately after being dropped off?

> Wish they were smarter?

> Skip school to eat pizza at the local pizza joint?

> Shoot each other with BB Guns?

> Sabotage the water heater in their house to flood the whole basement, causing thousands of dollars in damage?

> Fall in love with the neighbor girl, then find out she likes your friend, not you?

> Wish for a different family?

> Hate gym class?

> Steal Christmas cards out of mailboxes, steam them open, take the money out, then put them back?

> Love to swim?

> Let the neighbor's barking dog out of the yard in hopes that it will run away?

> Sneak out of the house late at night to attempt to ride their bike ten miles to a party, only to be picked up by the police and taken right back home?

> Ask to sit in a different part of the plane so they can ask the adult next to them for alcohol?

> Love their grandparents more than their actual parents?

> Rig the school election?

> Get good at fixing cigarette burns in carpet?

> Throw rocks at cars, then when the driver stops, you fire up the chainsaw you've brought along and chase the driver?

> Like "girls'" *and* "boys'" toys?

> Need help with their homework?

> Burn the field behind their house down?

> Get picked on?

> Point shotguns at their friends?

> Drink too much and lie down on their waterbeds?

> Steal cars?

> Sit in the back of class so as to not be noticed?

> Love the bus ride home from school because you're not in school *or* at home?

> Want to be writers?

My Diet

I have coffee for breakfast.

Booze for dinner.

Nothing for lunch.

See why I'm thinner?

Self
Portrait

Sewing Lessons

This morning I found out someone had sewn the legs
together on my pajamas.

I think it was the dog, because she likes my wife better
than me.

Or maybe it was my wife, because I like the dog more
than her.

But why sew the legs of my pajamas together? Who
has that kind of time? I don't think we even own a
sewing machine.

Didn't my daughter ask me for a needle and thread the
other day?

Steady as She Goes

I've forged no new paths.

The roads I take have already been driven on.

I am not an explorer.

I am not an adventurer.

I am not the guy in front with the machete.

I don't start the campfire.

I didn't wiggle my loose tooth.

I wasn't the one who popped the question.

I must get the swirl because I can't decide between chocolate and vanilla.

I order the first thing on the menu, which is mozzarella sticks.

I bought the first car at the dealer I saw, which turned out to be one of those vans modified to carry a handicapped person.

I am not handsome.

I am an average height.

I cry at sad movies and laugh at the comedies.

I am neither smart, nor dumb.

We've met before.

I'm Brad.

Stop, Drop, and Roll

If you are thrown out of a moving car, is it like in the movies?

Do you roll yourself up like a burrito?

Like a child rolling down a hill?

Has anyone seen *The Big Lebowski*? The ringer!

I worked with a guy named Josh. He intrigued me with a story about pushing someone out of a moving car.

I think his reasoning revolved around drugs. Maybe someone owed him money? Maybe he was a maniac who liked that sort of thing. Maybe I could have asked for more details? It probably would have made a better story.

Sure, You Can Borrow My Stereo

To my friend Tim, I bestowed:

The use of my stereo, whenever he wanted.

And to this day, that note he has flaunted.

The date I put was February 30th.

To this day, it has caused quite a tiff.

I keep waiting for that day to come.

Though it is true I was quite dumb.

He laughed as I asked for it politely.

So then, I surveilled his house nightly.

But when I could not find the note, I burn down his
house for good measure.

You might think that was heavy handed.

And then, I was remanded.

So, kids, don't write notes when you are high.

Perhaps I should clarify.

Burning down your friend's house to get a note back
isn't cool.

The upside was, in jail they let me finish high school.

Take that Adrian High!

Through the Ages

My dad sold my bike when I was 8.

My mom sold my car when I was 17.

A guy stole my wallet when I was 21.

A woman named Laura broke my heart when I was 30.

My wife sold my house when I was 40.

I died when I was 43.

I came back as a zombie when I was 44.

Got remarried when I was 45.

Villagers chased me when I was 46.

They cut my head off.

I'm now in a jar on a mantle.

I'm bored.

Trifecta

I was made redundant.

Then I spent an abundant,

amount on a horse named,

John Denver's Ghost.

He fell in the stretch.

I lost, and I wretched.

Next time, I'll do something smart.

Like play the lotto.

Who Are You Again?

I worked with this guy called Sam.

I think maybe it was Dan.

Though now he's called Sue.

Sorry, *she* is still kind of new.

But I didn't hear this firsthand.

So, Sue could still be Dan.

Maybe I'll call Karyn and ask.

Wait, it's Karen, right?

PART THREE

The Lull

The middle of the record

A Limerick

I once knew a man from Macon.

If you think this is a limerick, you are mistaken.

His brother's wife learned

(who had a large bosom, which he so yearned)

that they liked to play a game called "which hole does

the snake go in?"

Are People Still Nice?

I spent a lot of my thirties planning motorcycle trips. Some panned out, some didn't. Toward the end of one particular journey, Tim and I were making a stop in Memphis, TN. We had a few stops to make while there: Graceland, Sun Records, the usual music related stuff. Not that I had any idea what to expect at Graceland *or* Sun Studio. There was a scene in the movie *This Is Spinal Tap* where they are standing near Elvis's grave in Graceland and singing (badly) one of his songs. This was all I had to go on. Even though I have played music my whole life, I am a terrible music historian.

There had been a brief rain storm a few minutes outside of Memphis, and we just caught the edge of it. Getting caught out in the rain on a motorcycle can be a stressful thing, with brief rainstorms or light showers being the worst. If it doesn't rain enough to pull the gunk up from the road and then wash it away, you're left with a slippery street and the potential for a crash, and a brief storm over Memphis is what we were rolling into.

Tim and I pulled off the highway and stopped at the bottom of the ramp. First stop, Graceland. We needed to take a left turn onto a busy four-lane divided road. I headed out first and made it halfway through my turn before I lost it, a slow-motion tumble onto my left side. Tim confirmed later that it was indeed in slow motion; it seemed to take forever for me to fall over. Tim pulled around me and over to the side of the road. My old Yamaha was heavier than usual because of the way Tim and I traveled—self-sufficient. While we of course sampled the local cuisine where we went, we liked to have everything on the bikes we'd need, including one trip when my bike wasn't running well and I had to purchase a dozen spark plugs from a local Yamaha dealer somewhere in Mississippi. The bike runs on two.

Bypassing the self-injury assessment, I went straight to getting the bike upright and getting my ass out of the road. The other light must have turned green, because traffic started coming toward me. I was in the middle of the two lanes, blocking traffic—shit. I heaved at the bike but couldn't get it upright, I glanced over to where I thought Tim had ridden, and I could see he was working on getting off, getting unhooked and pried out of and away from his bike. The cars were inching closer. I heaved but I just couldn't get it upright, and I waited for help, maybe someone in one of those cars inching toward me. It was obvious I needed help, and if I never got the bike upright, I think they would have just run me over. Why wasn't anyone coming to help, dammit? Where were the people of Memphis to help me out?

Tim finally made it over, and we quickly got the bike upright and into neutral, and pushed over to the side of the road next to his bike. Damage assessments to me and the bike needed to now take place. My left leg hurt, but it didn't seem to be any more than something that would be a little black and blue the next day. The main problem was that my clutch lever was broken. Getting to see Elvis's grave was the least of my worries now.

This was early internet browser on your phone days. Blackberry days. Tim was the man at working that thing, and after several minutes we found a shop that thought they might have a part that would work. I removed the rest of my broken clutch, and we pushed the bike a short way into a hotel parking lot, which we thought we might just need if we couldn't find the right part. So, off Tim went, while I waited there. It's not a great feeling to see your riding partner go off without you. Makes one feel abandoned. It was maybe thirty minutes before Tim was back, clutch lever in hand. It wasn't perfect, since it was for a different bike, but dammit if it didn't work perfectly. I was so relieved.

Off we went to Graceland, which turned out to be a bust. It was crazy expensive to get in, so we just checked out the lobby, marveled at all the Asian tourists, and left. You can see Elvis's plane from the parking lot, for God's sake! Next was a trip to Sun Studio, and we were both put off by a guy just hanging out in the lobby, playing guitar and singing. It seemed like he worked there? I have no love for that sort of thing. It's one of the things that make me not get along with other musicians. Same story at Sun—too expensive for the tour. Tim and I weren't so much frugal as we were poor. We're also idiots, but not suckers.

Friends Like These

I recently connected with an old friend named Rick.

Who admits that when he was younger, he was a dick.

I thought he was alright.

Until he pulled that knife on me that night.

Jesus, I guess he was a prick?

Never Stop

I moved back to Michigan after living in Virginia for a short time. I was determined to get back into writing and playing music live. I had not been on any sort of stage in front of people for more than ten years. The first call I made was to my friend and longtime music partner, Tim. He was immediately in. I bought myself a $100 acoustic guitar off eBay and got to work writing songs. On top of the bad stuff I began to write, we learned a few more and practiced, practiced, practiced.

I moved into a small upstairs apartment in the town Tim and I grew up in. Like a gift from the lord above, there was a coffee shop about a block away that held an open mic night. Now, we had an actual goal. We scoped the place out for a couple weeks to make sure the vibe was positive and that if we failed miserably, we would be welcomed back. Kind of important.

A couple of songs in our pocket after all this practicing and we were ready to step onstage. *The* week came, we put our name on the sheet, and the triumphant return of Latin Love Baskets was going to happen. Can it be triumphant if no one knew we were gone? Or back?

Our time slot came, and wracked with nerves we jumped back into the live music pool. There were probably fifteen to twenty people there to watch as we made our way to the front corner of the coffee shop, which was now doubling as the stage, Tim with his lyrics and harmonica and me with my $100 acoustic Ibanez guitar. First song, no problem. Second song, problem. In the middle of the song, my guitar pick slipped out of my hand and I subsequently stopped playing to reach down and pick it up. I stopped. The number one rule in playing live: don't stop. If we were practicing and I had dropped my pick and stopped, it would have been fine, but here, in front of a non-enthusiastic, non-paying audience, it was pretty disgraceful. I know it sounds like I am overreacting, and I assure you, I am.

I am not a professional musician. It is not nor has it ever been my livelihood. What I want is to put on a good show, to give someone who might just be starting out inspiration to go home and pick up their instrument, to be proficient at my craft. I expect a lot of myself, I know. But if I don't, who will?

Pffft, Sports

I was never good at sports. In my late teens, I figured out I was okay at downhill skiing, but bad at everything else. In eighth grade, all the boys participated in football, so I gave it a go. I was bad. We can gloss over the fact that I didn't have proper football cleats and wore my high-top Converse All Stars, which might have been pink. I may have been mistaken for a girl on the team, now that I think about it. Another blow to my already low popularity in school.

I lasted all of one game, or maybe it was a scrimmage before the actual first game of the season. I was given the position called "Safety." This is the farthest away from the action on the defense. I was the last person to stop an opposing player should they get through the other ten players on the team. I can only assume that the coach believed that since all the plays were running plays, it was unlikely they would get through all ten people and thus hinge on my tackling them. Well, this is exactly what happened. The other team did a running play, and the player got through all ten people and then ran over the eleventh, me, and scored a touchdown. I apologized and received words of encouragement, which I'm sure was just shouting from the coach about how terrible of a job I'd done. So, the coach gave me another chance. I was ready this time. The same thing happened. I was the last one to try and tackle the same guy, and he ran over me. I went to the next game and the coach wisely left me on the bench to watch. After that, I quit. My football career was over.

My only other foray into sports was an attempt to play soccer in my mid-teens. I remember a lot of running and a couple of inter-team scrimmages. All this running was getting in the way of my smoking though, so I made the obvious choice and quit that bullshit soccer team.

I was done with team sports. Solo ventures were for me. I would either succeed, or fail, alone. I understood music because I felt there was beauty in it; sports always seemed chaotic, messy, and violent. Kind of like that crazy free-form jazz I come across every now and then, but with extra tackling.

I am mediocre at snow skiing, skateboarding, and racing my motorcycle. Don't worry though, I have the participation trophies to prove it.

Sleepy

I knew a drummer who could keep a beat.

But in between songs, he liked to sleep.

Truth be told,

we thought he was just old,

until I found an empty bottle of Vicodin in my

loveseat.

The Rocket

"Three… Two… One… Go!.."

It's silent inside my helmet as I shout the countdown. I hold a tight grip on the mechanical levers I've created to control the roll, pitch, and yaw. Nothing happens. I wait for a few more seconds. Nothing. I look over at my wife approximately twenty feet away, foot hovering over the starter, a frightened look on her face. She can't hear me.

I start the countdown again, with my fingers this time. Three… Two… One… I throw her the thumbs up, then face forward. I wait a few seconds, nothing.

I again look in my wife's direction and she's stomping on the foot switch. She looks up and throws up her hands. *I don't know,* she mouths. I give her the okay sign with my fingers, then hold up my palm to signal her to stop. She backs away from the footswitch as I begin to unbuckle my harness.

Test Flight One, scrubbed.

It's been eighteen months since the initial 1.0 plans were crudely drawn; I am currently on 6.3a. Clearly, I have a lot more work to do.

It has cost me thousands of dollars, a welding class at my local community college, six months as a part-time journeyman electrician, more hours than I care to count hanging out at model rocket shows, forty-one emails back and forth with retired NASA engineer Michael Witcombe, and two threats of divorce.

When I was nine, I watched the Space Shuttle Columbia lift off from Kennedy Space Center in Florida. My life was changed forever, and it culminated with me strapping myself to a homemade rocket on a beautiful June morning in 2018.

6.3a – failed. I winched my craft back into the workspace, aka my shed, and begin the painstaking process of checking over the wiring, electronics, and physical well-being of my project. I had roughly 450 feet of 14/3 Romex to look over, ten Dyson Animal 2 vacuum motors to inspect, and twenty-two Cesaroni P54-6G Dual Thrust rocket motors: twenty for flight, two for landing. This was going to take some time.

June turned into July, which slipped into August. I had concluded after weeks of investigation that I had a firewire initiator. I ordered a few more and reran the troublesome one, and two others that looked suspect. A new launch date of September 2 was set. V6.5b was set for Test Flight Two.

The morning was cooler than I had hoped, so I pushed the launch from 9 a.m. to 1 p.m. I had a light lunch of tuna pasta salad (w/ olive oil mayo) and suited up. When I locked my Kirby Morgan diving helmet into the collar, the world goes silent. Stepping out my back door reminds of walking out on a cold winter morning after a heavy snowfall. Tranquil, maybe even like stepping foot onto the moon must have felt. Though without all the gravity or fear of death thing. This helped keep me calm on what I hoped would be a momentous day.

After the last failed launch and slight confusion, I came up with a series of hand gestures to eliminate that issue on the second launch. I ended up sketching out hand gestures, printed and laminated on card stock. All my testing with communication devices compatible with the helmet and that had proper range failed the vibration testing. I'm expecting some serious vibration on liftoff and through stage one and two of the engine burn. We'll be going very low-tech for pre-launch communication.

With my wife and child safely inside our sunroom, I strap myself in. Before tightening down my five-point harness, I need to test the Dyson motors. One of the changes I have made since June is the ability to run a pre-flight test on the Dysons via a separate rocker switch on my small dash. The Dysons are there for stability. I had to buy sixteen Dyson Animal 2 motors to come up with ten that could output the same volume of air. I flip the rocker, and though I can't hear the motors whirl to life, I installed a red LED that allows me to physically see if they're operating. I can see five from my vantage point, so I look to my wife and she shows me five fingers and then the okay. I switch off the Dyson motors and begin my final preparations.

With all looking good, I'm ready for my final countdown. After I hold up a single finger, she will begin the one-minute countdown. At ten seconds, she will flip on a red light attached to a post some fifteen feet straight in front of me. At five seconds, the Dysons should come up. When it hits three seconds, she will flip on a green light that sits directly under the red. My goal for today is 7,500 feet. I am ready.

I hold up a single finger and the one-minute countdown starts. I triple-check my harness and give everything I can see another visual inspection. The red light goes on. Immediately following that, the lights on the Dysons come up. Green Light. Three... Two... One...

In an instant, the Dyson nearest my right leg is ripped from its aluminum enclosure as the two Cesaroni motors fire it into the sky like a champagne cork. A second later, the enclosure holding the Dyson and the two rockets directly in front of me fires, sending the whole craft over backward with me staring up at the sky. Before I can process *that*, the enclosure that just flipped me backward comes loose and goes screaming over my head, through our fence, and into the adjacent woods. Unlike the first one that came off, I'll find remnants of this later. It will leave a scorched mark and plastic bits imbedded in an oak tree.

Launch number 2, craft 6.5b is a failure. I am unhurt, but the craft is damaged. For the third time in recent months, I am threatened with divorce. I can see the toll this is taking on my daughter, whose face is white as a sheet as I'm helped out of the craft. My dream needs to die, and I am at peace with that.

I sell most of the parts on eBay and make a few bucks back. I also write a book about my experience, though Michael Witcombe from NASA tells me I can't use his name. I don't think he wants to associate with my failures. The book is called *Dad, in Space*, and it's available in eBook and paperback now.

The following are a few notes from my rocket build journal.

Sorry, in advance, for the abysmal handwriting.

Parts list *

- 10 used Dyson Ball, Animal vacuums (ebay, CL)
- Romex - 250 ft 14/3 x 2
- cord/foot switch Ikea Lamp x 4
- Cesaroni- P54-6G Dual thrust motor x 20 (10k alt.) + ? for landing
- ignitor + starter
- Hanger strap - 100 ft.
- racing seat - used
- aluminum square tube 1" x 20 @ 6'
- welder
- Angle grinder
- Lithium Iron phosphat battery x 2
- wire connectors
- Kirby Morgan 37 w/ MWP $8k
- 4L oxygen bottle x 4
- Viking HD suit
- 5-point harness
- Bare X-mission Evolution Drysuit
- Mills manufacturing Cargo parachute

- Blue Sky Network Hawkeye 7200
  global GPS tracker
- Ford F-150 front coils- used
  ~~18~~ x 10
- Hardware Pack #1 ⎤ see
- Hardware Pack #2 ⎦ itemized
- Aerospace Logic 2-1/4 Altimeter 35k

* other ideas
  welding class at wcc
* Journeyman electrician (call Matt)
* need to file flight plan?
* flare gun?

motor, engine X2

coils?

← 2'

seat

power

out to motor

springs?

rg
g x
g
b
r
w
y
b

V1.

P54 X2

O. A2

V2.

P54 x2

O A2

V3

engine mounts further away

Time Well Spent

How do you spend your time?

- Texting?
- Eating?
- Moving?
- Writing?
- Killing?
- Foraging?
- Building?
- Running?
- Yelling?
- Cursing?
- Fixing?
- Dying?

Dying…

Flip Me Over

I wanted to write a story upside down.
No, no, not me. My feet are on the ground.
Really, my ass is in a chair.
If you turned the book around, you must care.
So, thanks for playing along, and here's hoping.
Now, flip the book around, and keep going.

Up in Arms

If you let the gorilla out of the zoo, will it go around
ripping people's arms off?

Is that just something people say?

What would its motivation be?

Revenge?

How different is it than a maniac running around with
a gun?

An animal being let out of a cage.

PART FOUR

By Proxy

Likely happened to someone else

No Hot Air Balloons

When I lived in Boulder, Colorado, I worked with a gal named Tiffany. I think we liked each other, but that's not relevant to this story. She told me a terribly sad tale about going for a ride in a hot air balloon with her long-time boyfriend—oh, let's call him John. Tiffany, John, and the balloonist go up, and it's a lovely day. Perfect, some would say. They are up floating around for a time, enjoying the scenery, when John asks Tiffany to marry him. He has the ring ready, spent the cash on the balloon, and got up the nerve to ask all while cruising around at two thousand feet.

But man, did John misread the situation, and the current level of commitment from his girlfriend. Poor John. Tiffany was nothing but honest though. She didn't give John a "how about I think about it and get back to you" or "John, I love you and this is a wonderful gesture, give me a day to think it over." Tiffany just told poor John, no. *No*, at two thousand feet, with an extra guy in the balloon. How about that for an uncomfortable ride down?

Maybe John should have jumped? Would that have made for a better ending to the story? Did you see it coming because I called it a sad tale at the start? I never met John and have only Tiffany's side of this story. Poor bastard.

That Time I Won a Car

So, you want to win a car? You find one of those big plexiglass boxes with the slit in the top located near the food court in the mall. Then you think, hey I could use a new Ford Mustang/Pontiac Firebird/Geo Tracker, so you enter. But then you have another great idea: I can only enter this contest once, so I should enter my buddy. Genius! No one actual wins these things anyway. The dealer just wants your info so they can sell you a car, later.

I'm sure if my friend wins, he'll give me the car, or maybe we can just sell the thing and split the money. What's fair here, 60/40? The 60% going to me, obviously. It's a win/win.

What is *not* factored in to my deciding to enter my friend is how badly money fucks things up. A free Ford Mustang is *no* exception. From here on out, we can call my friend Shaun, and to keep things simple, we'll just keep calling the car a Mustang. I mention the contest to Shaun a couple days later in casual conversation.

Fast forward a couple/few weeks, and Shaun calls and is delighted. "We won!" he shouts into the phone. "The car, can you believe it?" The *we* Shaun's referring to is, of course, he and I. This would turn into a worthwhile life lesson for me. Painful, but beneficial. We were still kids who weren't emotionally ready to deal with anything so grown up. It seemed too simple to me at the time: sell the car, split the profit. We started with nothing, and would come out with several thousand dollars apiece.

I pitched my idea to Shaun, who agreed this was a fair deal. I worked all my contacts to find a buyer for the Ford Mustang, which did not take long. I had a buyer who would pay $17,500 for a car that cost $22,000. I would then take $10,000, and Shaun for all his trouble would take $7,500. Easy, right?

A couple days out from picking the car up, driving it over to the buyer's house, and getting the money, the whole arrangement fell apart. What I failed to understand was how pleased Shaun's parents were about this new Ford Mustang. Shaun had been driving a car given to him by his parents, and with this new car, they were free to take the old one back and give it to his younger brother. Shaun had relayed none of this to me, and failed to communicate any of *our* deal to his parents. I was spending that $10K five times over; I simply did not understand that I was fucked, and about to be as broke as I had always been.

The deal was now restructured. Shaun and his father had worked with the car dealer to forgo the Ford Mustang for a cheaper car and some cash: a $12,500 Ford Escort and $3,000 in cash. Well, $3,000 is better than nothing, so I swallowed my anger and resentment and agreed. Enter Shaun's poor communication skills once again. Shaun had an agreement with his parents to split this money with me. They said it was more than fair, and I should be grateful that I was getting anything. Shaun *did* win the car after all. They had me dead to rights on that, I guess.

Shaun dropped off my $1,500 check, and we never spoke again. So, do yourself a favor and don't enter your friend, brother, mom, priest, or mistress into any contest. Just let the other guy win.

The Boat

When I was a young man, I met a nice girl.

Her only redeeming quality I can remember is she was tall.

I do like tall.

We had a date, it went well.

I introduced her to my friends.

That went well.

One of my friends realized they were related.

Cousins.

Small world.

The only other thing I remember is they shared an uncle who was pulling a boat on a trailer. The boat came off and killed someone. He went to prison.

PART FIVE

The Finally

Wrapping up

Spirit Animal

Southwestern Georgia, 2006

Tim and I were on a motorcycle trip. There are times during these trips where you make last-minute decisions to see a particular town or historical marker that takes you a hundred miles in a different direct than originally planned.

It was spring 2006, and we had landed at a campground in southwestern Georgia for the night. I can recall when this was because it was the spring following Hurricane Katrina, which ravaged the Gulf Coast. What we saw on this trip left a blemish on my soul. I wish we hadn't ridden the Gulf Coast that spring. I wish I could replace these memories of all the foundations without houses, destroyed restaurants, mounds of personal effects piled up on the side of the road, and displaced people who had lost everything. This story is not about what we saw, though, as I have no wish to relive what I saw on the Gulf Coast. It sounds insensitive to talk about how the sights impacted you without giving credit to those who actually lived through it.

Our trip was winding down, and we were heading back up to Atlanta; we had found another gem of a campground. The place was mostly empty, because it was early in the season, so we had a lovely spot right next to a lake.

The night was routine—we pitched our tents, had dinner (which probably came in a bag), and just hung out until bedtime. We may have even had a fire, though impromptu fires are often difficult because everyone scrounges the campground for wood. We'll give it a *maybe*.

The moon was luminous. It settled itself above the lake and lit our campsite exquisitely. Tim and I were weary. It had been a long day, and we needed some rest for the final push that would soon come.

A few hours later, I awoke, though it is not that uncommon for me to toss and turn during the night. I opened my eyes and was surprised by the amount of moonlight illuminating my tent; it was so bright I had a hard time reconciling the time. I noticed something. Wait, did I?

I lifted my head a little off what was categorized as a pillow but was a sorry excuse for one. I stared at the side of my tent. A shadow. A silhouette. Was it a rock? A bush? The fire ring? My eyes slid into focus, and I could clearly see the outline of an animal sitting just outside my tent.

I was startled. I raised myself up to my elbows, and being unsure of that else to do, I whisper-yelled, "Tim, Tim." The silhouette wasn't moving. "Tim." My voice was now raised and sounding a little panicked.

The silhouette moved. I now called out, "Tim, wake up man."

"What's up?" He was awake.

A little relieved, I blurted out, "There's an animal outside my tent, like right next to me." There was now rustling going on in Tim's tent, and I envisioned him getting up to investigate.

"It's moving." My voice was still coming out higher than it should have. I was still rattled. The animal had gotten up and started to walk away. It seemed in no great rush to go and was less frightened of me than I was of it.

"Did you say an animal?" Tim replied, as I heard him still rustling around in his tent, presumably putting something on. I heard the zipper on Tim's tent and moved from my elbows to a sitting position.

"Do you see it?" I cried out.

"I see it, I see it" Tim exclaimed.

Silence.

"Can you tell what it is?" I called out.

"No… I can't tell. A coyote? Dog maybe?" he said.

"Fuck me," I uttered. I collapsed back down onto my pillow. "What the hell was that about?"

Tim was chuckling as he went back inside his tent and zipped it back up. It came off as more of a nervous chuckle though. We chatted for a couple minutes about what just happened, and then Tim said, "It was your spirit animal."

"My what?" I spat back.

"Your spirit animal, man," Tim said with all seriousness. "We all have one—that must have been yours."

I lay there staring at the ceiling of my tent, thinking about what Tim had said. I was not sure if he had just made that up, or if this was something he'd read. Maybe we covered this in college when we had Native American Literature together.

I have always found this story to be hard to tell. It's nearly impossible to slip it into a casual conversation. "Did you say spirit animal?" I can just hear someone saying. Or does it become a camping story? "You'll never guess what happened to me while camping this one time."

I don't know what the animal was. The silhouette appeared to be somewhere between a coyote and a dog, and Tim's glimpse on that moonlit night could get us no closer to knowing.

Maybe I'll see it again, someday. Perhaps it *was* my spirit animal sent to help guide me. Tim had told me around this time in our lives that "it's half over." Is it foolishness to think my animal was sent to show me my halfway point?

I hope to see you again, my friend. My guide.

Eulogy for my Father

I want to speak at my father's funeral; I think I have a pretty good bit. My father has always been crazy about bicycles. For reference, please re-read my story titled: "Have You Seen My Bike?" Though, that is hardly a complete representation of his love and passion for this two-hundred-year-old transportation contraption. My father has always had multiple bikes, and I've always respected the fact that he rode miles to work for years. It is impressive.

The Eulogy:

remember, this is a somber event, not a comedy show

My father *(pause)* was a genius.
Maybe it will surprise some of you to hear me say that, but he was.
I was able to have a conversation with my father about anything. Anything.

The poetry of Robert Frost, the political structure of
The Republic of Ireland vs. Northern Ireland, which is
the best hammer drill to buy, or even, "Hey, I have this
weird rash on my arm, any idea what it might be?"

(short pause)

Impressive, right?

(short pause)

But some of you are looking a little puzzled. You
might be thinking, "That doesn't sound like the Gary I
knew, or remember."

But you are wrong, you knew him as well, if not better
than I did.

So, let me explain.

(short pause)

The genius of my father wasn't in having intricate
knowledge about political structures, literature, home
improvement, or obscure medical procedures.

His genius was, and there can be no other word for it,
it was in steering any conversation pertaining to any
topic, to bicycles.

(pause for laughs)

My father and I were once having a conversation about
my wife filing for divorce after ten years of marriage,

161

and the next thing I know, we're talking about how there was this classic Pinarello bike that just showed up at the shop.

On the drive home I'd think, how did he do that? Did I even finish my story about my wife divorcing me?

(short pause)

The way he worked parties was masterful. I once saw a thirteen-year-old boy hand money over to him *at his own bar mitzvah* because after five minutes talking to my dad, he wanted to help with improvements to the bike shop.

(short pause)

Any conversation. Any topic.

It was one of the things about him that I loved. That *we* loved.

On behalf of the family, I want to thank you all for coming today, it means a lot to me, Mary, Brian, and Clint.

(short pause)

And as a postscript, I want to let you all know that we've melted down several of my father's bikes to make this beautiful urn you see here.

(point to urn and pause for laughs)

Sorry, I couldn't resist.

Thanks again everyone.

One Last Big One

It's noon, on a foggy Saturday in December. I am in what appears to be a long, narrow storeroom, listening to two doctors talk about a local restaurant they want to try. I can't comprehend where I am or how I ended up here. Perhaps I was abducted several days ago and my blindfold was just taken off? I am wearing a disposable hospital gown but don't remember putting it on.

I look around the storeroom and contemplate stealing something to aid in my escape. There is nothing worth taking. I think I will have to fight my way out.

I go back to listening to the conversation the two doctors are having in the other room about the restaurant, and I then realize I've been there. The pea soup was good, salty, with just the right amount of ham.

I look toward the open door. Was it open before? Did that just happen? Maybe I can slip out without those doctors noticing. Do I have my clothes on under this gown? The clock on the wall in front of me says

12:04. Is that p.m. or a.m.? It has a loud "tick, tick, tick." Was this purchased at Target, or ordered via some hospital supply company? Is this a hospital I'm in?

There's no time to waste, I stand up to begin my escape. I'm unsteady. *Dizzy.* I hear footsteps coming, so I quickly sit back down. Shit! I look back up at the clock and it's 12:05, and I ask myself the same initial question: Where am I?

The footsteps stop; they are close. I don't have anything to defend myself with. *Shit!*

"Mr. Poore?" I'm staring at the clock on the wall. I think I am swaying back and forth a little.

"Yes?" I reply without looking in her direction. Her? Tick, tick, tick.

"You can come with me, they're ready for you."

I take a quick mental inventory of her age, weight, and height. I can take her. I wonder if she has her car keys on her—I'm going to need those. I begin to follow her down a wide, empty hallway. This must be a hospital, but what kind? Psychiatric?

"How are you holding up?" she asks. I don't

answer, and we just walk in silence for several seconds.

"Here we are." Her tone is melancholy. She is gesturing toward an open door on her right. I walk through obediently. My wife is here, along with a dozen doctors. My daughter is being born today. How can that be? It's December. She was due in March.

Whatever functioning parts of my brain are still operating stop. Mandatory shutdown is required.

www.ingramcontent.com/pod-product-compliance
Lightning Source LLC
Chambersburg PA
CBHW070321120726
47909CB00008B/2542